The
Cosmic Camp
Caper

Time for cAMP !

Signature

Books by Robert Elmer

www.elmerbooks.org

ASTROKIDS

PROMISE OF ZION

ADVENTURES DOWN UNDER

THE YOUNG UNDERGROUND

ROBERT ELMER

AstroKids

The Cosmic Camp Caper

BETHANY BACKYARD®

www.bethanyhouse.com

The Cosmic Camp Caper
Copyright © 2001
Robert Elmer

Cover and text illustrations by Paul Turnbaugh
Cover design by Lookout Design Group, Inc.

Scripture quotations are from the *International Children's Bible, New Century
Version,* copyright © 1986, 1988 by Word Publishing, Dallas, Texas 75039. Used
by permission.

Published by Bethany House Publishers
A Ministry of Bethany Fellowship International
11400 Hampshire Avenue South
Bloomington, Minnesota 55438
www.bethanyhouse.com

Printed in the United States of America by
Bethany Press International, Bloomington, Minnesota 55438

Library of Congress Cataloging-in-Publication Data
Elmer, Robert.
    The cosmic camp caper / by Robert Elmer.
        p. cm. —(AstroKids ; 6)
Summary: While the gang from *CLEO*-7 imagines roasting marshmallows over
miniature volcanoes and practicing laser archery, Camp Little Dipper proves to be
something else entirely.
    ISBN 0-7642-2361-5 (pbk.)
    [1. Space stations—Fiction. 2. Camps—Fiction. 3. Christian life—Fiction.
4. Science fiction.] I. Title.
    PZ7.E4794 Co 2001
    [Fic]—dc21   2001003950

To Pastor Jon and Linda Aldrich—

it's time for camp!

Robert

Freckles

ROBERT ELMER is an Earth-based author who writes for life-forms all over the solar system. He and his family and their dog, Freckles, live about ninety-three million miles from the sun, or three hundred ninety-one million miles from Jupiter. That's a long way! If you could somehow drive that far (and of course you couldn't), it would take about six hundred eighty-six years to cover the distance. And that's not even stopping for gas on Mars!

Contents ✱ ✱ ✱

MEET THE
AstroKids

Lamar "Buzz" Bright

Show the way, Buzz! The leader of the AstroKids always has a great plan. He also loves Jupiter ice cream.

Daphne "DeeBee" Ortiz

DeeBee's the brains of the bunch—she can build or fix almost anything. But, suffering satellites, don't tell her she's a "GEEN-ius"!

Theodore "Tag" Ortiz

Yeah, DeeBee's little brother, Tag, always tags along. Count on him to say something silly at just the wrong time. He's in orbit.

Kumiko "Miko" Sato

Everybody likes Miko the stowaway. They just don't know how she got to be a karate master, or how she knows so much about space shuttles.

Vladimir "Mir" Chekhov

So his dad's the station commander and Mir usually gets his way? Give him a break! He's trying. And whatever he did, it was probably just a joke.

① Shuttle Trouble ✳ ✳ ✳

I knew we were in trouble the first time we saw the Camp Little Dipper space bus.

Big trouble.

I mean, I had been on a few rickety old spaceships before. Even antiques from way back in the twenty-first century.

But this had to be the mother of all space wrecks. Thruster tubes pointed every which way. Bent landing legs looked like they would break when they touched down in shuttle hangar 02. And the paint job was so burnt you could hardly read the painted red letters on the side: *Camp Little Dipper*.

This *thing* was going to take us from our space station home to three great weeks of camp?

Right. Just look at the space maps: From here on *CLEO-7*, we would head out seventy-eight million kilometers, then slingshot past Mars.

But watch it! We'd have to keep our shields up through the asteroid belt. Then we'd zoom another five hundred fifty million kilometers to Io ("EYE-oh"), one of Jupiter's twenty-eight moons. That's where the camp was.

I was worrying about all that as we watched the space camp bus shut down its engines.

FOOOO-ahhhh-sssss, poppa-poppa-pop.

Meanwhile, our station's big shuttle hangar doors closed.

Ka-THUNK.

I looked at DeeBee. DeeBee looked at me. And we were probably both thinking the same thing: *No way. This is not at all like what we saw on the camp holo-vid we watched with our folks.*

"The other shuttle's in the shop for repairs," explained the driver, a frumpy-looking older guy with a name tag that said *Gus A. Paulow*. He kicked at a fold-out stepladder that didn't quite fold out.

Right. We were stuck with the shuttle supremo.

"Whose idea was this, anyway?" asked my friend Mir. Mir knew whose idea it was. He finished off a space dog with extra ketchup, licked his fingers, and laughed.

"Just kidding, Buzz. Just kidding."

"Well, it seemed like a good idea at the time." My mouth was dry, and my palms were sweaty. What we needed now was a good, late-model time-travel machine to take us back about a month ago. You'd think that by the year 2175 they could have invented something like that.

I wish.

Yeah, if I could just slip back a month or so, before I got the brainstorm that all the AstroKids should go to Camp Little Dipper. I would have kept my big mouth shut!

"Too late now." That was DeeBee. She was a "GEEN-ius," as her little brother, Tag, always reminded us. She held on to his hand. Miko, who had been really jazzed about going to camp, still looked ready to go. And MAC, DeeBee's floating drone, grabbed a bag with one of his hands and picked up Zero-G, the dog, with the other.

"You and I are not allowed on this trip," complained Zero-G. "Let me down, if you please!"

So that's what MAC did. *Clunk.* Of course, I couldn't blame MAC. He knew we all wished they could come with us.

But I couldn't worry about it, not just then. Because all of a sudden, my stomach was doing funny things. You know, flips and turns. Serious butter-flies.

"Lamar?" My mother looked at me when I made for the door.

I waved back and tried to smile.

"I'll . . . be . . . right . . . back."

Well, what would *you* say, in front of all those moms and dads and everybody else? "I'm going to the rest room to throw up, Mom. Be right back"?

Right. It was way too late to chicken out now. But just tell that to my tummy.

"Are you all right, Master Buzz?"

Zero-G stepped on my heels. At least it wasn't my mom.

"I'm fine," I told him. Is a lie really a lie if you're talking to a dog?

QUESTION 01:

Wait a minute. Do you mean the *dog* was talking? That can't be right.

ANSWER 01:

Sure it is! Zero-G has an M2V (Mind to Voice) box on his collar, which reads his thoughts and says them in a nifty, Englishbutler-style voice. DeeBee put it together. Check out our adventures in the *Wired Wonder Woof* to find out how that happened.

Anyway, Zero-G wasn't buying it. The door went *swoop* as he nosed his way into the washroom behind me.

"You are *not* fine," he told me.

How could he tell? Maybe he could see the look on my face.

"Thanks, Doctor G." I took a deep breath. This was embarrassing. But what could I do about it?

Lift-Off!
2 (Barely)

$* * *$

"I always throw up when I get nervous, too."
Zero-G, my talking-dog friend, licked my hand.
"Perhaps you just need a chum."

Chum? That meant *buddy*, in Zero-G-speak.

"Thanks." I didn't want to look like a homesick
baby. Especially since we hadn't even left the station yet. "I wish you could come with us to Camp
Little Dipper. But the camp vid said no pets."

"Har-umph." Zero-G turned to leave the washroom. "There must be a way."

"I wish. But you take care of things here while
I'm gone, okay?"

"Don't fret about a thing, Master Buzz. Now,
you'd best be going before they leave without you."

I was done tossing my cookies. So I hurried
back to the shuttle hangar and looked for my duffel
bag. Where had I put it?

"No wrist interfaces, no zipsuits, no . . ." Mr.

Gus, the camp bus driver, was laying down the law.

Mir had to empty his bag of all his gadgets.

"Are you sure?" I think Mir just wanted to check. "Because in the vid, it says—"

"Sorry." Gus waved him off like a Plutonian fruit fly. "You must have watched last year's vid. Come on, kids. We still have to pick up a few others on *CLEO-5*."

Me? All I had packed for camp was—Whoa! My duffel bag seemed to have grown. Good thing every-thing was weightless in the shuttle hangar. Did Mom pack me an extra set of high-gravity shirts?

Too late to check. I zipped the end shut and schlepped to the bus.

Old Gus was checking his controls and must have decided we were late. Because all of a sudden, he started punching buttons and firing up the shuttle bus.

Whoopity-whoopity-ziiing! One of the thrusters started doing snap-crackle-pops.

I jumped through the door just in time. It started cranking shut.

"Be a good boy, Lamar!" hollered my mom, and I turned to wave. Oh great! She was crying.

"Where's Zero-G?" Tag pressed his nose to the blue plexi-window.

"I told him good-bye," I said.

"Find a seat!" yelled Gus. He whumped on a control panel with the palm of his hand before it squawked and sputtered. Looked as if he'd done that before.

Outside, Mom was still crying . . . something about me growing up too fast. If she kept that up, pretty soon I would be blubbering, too.

"Remember to say your prayers," she told me through the door.

I checked out Gus in the pilot's seat. He kicked at a flight panel in front of him. It spit back a shower of sparks before blinking on. Remembering to pray on *this* trip would not be a problem.

Whoo-whoo-weee . . . went the thrusters. Then something below us popped and poofed again. Everybody outside backed away from a cloud of black smoke. That's when the shuttle's outside door finally slammed, and the floor started to shake.

"How about that." Gus sounded surprised. "Lift-off."

I fell into my seat as the floor tipped one way, then the other. This was going to be better than the

Asteroid Revenge ride at Lunarland Amusement Park. (You know, on Earth's moon?)

At least, that's what I told myself as I looked out through my round window and waved again.

I wiped my eyes. "It's all that smoke . . ." I whispered to Mir, but that wasn't quite true.

"This is going to be cool!" whooped Tag.

Right. But I wasn't so sure.

"Hey, kid!" hollered Gus. He looked my way and pointed to a cluster of green glowing bubbles hanging down through a hole in the ceiling. "See those antimatter pods up there?"

Was that what they were? I ducked another shower of sparks.

"Hold 'em together, will you? Those pods come apart, and this whole thing's likely to exp . . ."

I didn't hear the rest of what Gus told me.

I was too busy holding those antimatter pods together.

And I had a feeling it was going to be a long trip to Io.

A very long trip.

3 Asteroid Attack ✳ ✳ ✳

"Mr. Gus!" yelled DeeBee. "Look out for that asteroid belt!"

Yikes! Miko put her hands over her face. Mir squeezed his eyes shut. My knuckles turned white on the seat in front of me.

"Eh? What's that?" Our driver looked back over his shoulder as if he had been taking us out for a nice Sunday-afternoon orbit.

I pointed. We were headed straight for an elephant-sized rock that was about to—

QUESTION 02:

Wait, wait! Asteroid belt? Is that something you wear?

ANSWER 02:

Almost. The asteroid belt is a huge layer of space junk between Mars and Jupiter. It's got gazillions of rocks, from micro-tiny to space station size. And if Gus's asteroid bumper-shields didn't work, this elephant-sized rock was going to put an elephant-sized hole through us.

"Relax." Gus grinned and whacked a control panel.

Deee-OOP! Our bumper-shields bumped the asteroid out of the way—just barely.

"Ohhh." Mir watched the asteroid scrape the side of the shuttle. "That was pretty close."

It was like that all the way through the belt. *Bumpity-thump-BUMP!*

"How about some snacks?" Gus called out.

"Nooooo!" most of us groaned. We were too busy trying to keep our breakfasts down.

"No kidding? Snacks?" Leave it to Mir to be hungry! "What have you got?"

Me, I kept my nose glued to the window, watching asteroids, holding my breath, trying not to think about food.

But it took hours before the bumping stopped. Eight and a half, to be exact. Finally, it was calm enough to unswitch my seat lock (that's the force field that held me in place).

"Ahh, finally." I stretched out my arms and legs, my body floated up, and I pretended to fly.

Yes! That was better.

And there it was.

Jupiter.

"Whoa." Mir saw it, too.

"Cool," whispered DeeBee.

Ditto. Who wouldn't think it was awesome? And who could miss the biggest planet in God's solar system? Big, stormy, and mean looking. We flew closer and closer, until it filled up our windows. I looked for the moons.

"One, two, three . . ." Tag was counting them, too. There would be twenty-eight, but half of 'em must have been hiding on the other side.

QUESTION 03:

How many did you say?

ANSWER 03:

Twenty-eight. Yup. Elara and Metis. Thebe and Ananke. Callisto and Io. Lots more. Want me to tell you how to pronounce those names?

QUESTION 04:

Uh ... why don't we just get on with the story?

ANSWER 04:

Gotcha.

"Iowa head," said our pilot.

"I've never been to Iowa." Tag wrinkled his nose. "DeeBee, what's an Iowa head?"

"No, no," explained his sister. "That's the moon called *Io*. And it's *ahead*. Io ... ahead. Get it?"

Got it. A couple of landing boosters cut in as she was talking. Twenty minutes later, we were swooping down on the most amazing-looking moon you've ever seen.

Think of our own moon, or maybe the Arizona desert, back on Earth. We're talking big canyons. Jaggy mountains. Huge volcanoes.

And in the middle of everything: a giant, see-through blue dome. Not like a sports dome. Way bigger. You could grow a huge city under this puppy. It even had a couple mountains inside.

"Camp Little Dipper?" I asked.

Gus nodded yes.

Then we:

a) Swooped in lower

b) Set down on a little flat strip

c) Coasted through a tunnel

d) Watched big doors swoosh shut behind us.

Finally, we all crawled out of the shuttle and looked around. Whew! Safe! God was listening to our prayers, that's for sure.

"Whooo-WEE!" Tag took a deep breath of dry, dusty air. And yeah, it felt pretty good to wiggle our wobbly legs again.

"Whasamatter?" Gus smiled and patted the side of his ship. "Didn't think old Bessie would make it?"

"Oh, it's not *that*, Mr. Gus." Miko was always polite.

"So, welcome to Camp Little Dipper!"

I wobbled around and took it all in.

We were in a bowl canyon, with rugged red hills all around. Here and there, a cactus dotted the landscape. Off in the distance, I could hear a waterfall. And then we saw the pink moonstone lodge, built right into the side of the canyon.

"Is that where we're going to live?" Mir wanted to know.

"Nope." Gus plugged an ion recharge hose into the nose of his shuttle and pointed to a dozen little beehive-shaped cabins, just below the lodge. "Human children sleep over there."

✻ ✻ ✻

Fast-forward thirty-two minutes and twelve seconds later. I was trying out my bunk in Cabin 02. Looked okay to me. It's just that one of my cabin mates never stopped talking from the minute we walked in.

"Name's Donny . . . *chew, pop* . . . Quantum." The name sounded kind of familiar. I shook his *biiig* hand. Who knew how many pieces of Galaxy Goop Double Bubble Gum he'd stuffed in his mouth?

"And you're going to want to . . . *chew* . . . check out my stock." We watched him pull out an expando bag from his pocket, like a wallet.

Fwop-fwop! It unstuffed on his bunk into the size of a big suitcase.

Cool.

And his *stock*? You've never seen so much candy

in your life! Pluto Pops. Tart-ee Stars. Choco-Planets. Luna Licorice . . .

Want me to go on?

"All they have at the camp store is . . . *chew, pop* . . . *healthy* stuff." Donny had a bubble going as big as his face. "And I've already checked out the camp . . . *chew, chew* . . . food."

"Pretty good?" Mir licked his lips.

"You kidding?" Donny worked his Galaxy Goop bubble and gave us a big thumbs-down. He is the only guy I've ever met who could talk and blow bubbles at the same time. It was a pretty good trick. "You're going to . . . *chomp, grind* . . . thank me for saving your life."

Right.

He went on. "And I'll tell you . . . *smack, chew* . . . something else."

We leaned in to hear.

"There's something really weird with the counselors."

"What do you mean?" I asked. Weird?

He just shrugged. "I dunno. *Popple, smack.* Just really odd. You'll see."

Hmm. I supposed we would.

He held up a ChocoPlanet. "But never mind.

Smackity, pop. Tell me what kind of candy you want. If I don't have it, I'll—hey, what's that? YEOW!"

I didn't think a guy built like Donny Quantum could move so fast. But you should have seen him launch when he saw my duffel bag wiggle and squirm, right by his feet.

Wait a minute.

Wiggle? Squirm?

Yikes!

Welcome to Camp
4 Little Dipper ✳ ✳ ✳

We found out what the wiggle and squirm in my duffel bag was. No wonder it was so heavy.

Three guesses. And no, it *wasn't* extra underwear.

"I say, it was a bit stuffy in that bag," said Zero-G. He wiggled out, sniffed the air, and looked around. "But it doesn't smell much better out here. Horrible, in fact. I have never cared for the smell of batteries."

"Batteries?" I asked. "Huh?"

"Oh, never mind. We don't seem to have any cats to chase, either. Pity. And what—"

"What are you *doing* here, Zero-G?"

"He stowed away!" chirped Tag.

"Is that what you call it?" Zero-G looked at me sideways. "I just thought you might need a chum."

"Whoa." Donny whistled. "You guys are going to catch it good. No pets allowed at camp."

"Just like no *candy* is allowed at camp?" Tag jumped to our dog's defense.

Donny frowned. "That's . . . *chew, smack* . . . different."

"I don't think so." I had an idea. "But we'll make you a deal."

"What kind of deal?"

"We won't tell about your candy, if you keep quiet about our pet."

"I assure you, my good man. I am most surely *not* a pet." Zero-G sat down and scratched.

Okay. I admit this felt kind of sneaky. But what else could we do? Send Zero-G home?

"Deal?" I held out my hand.

"Hmmm. Okay." Donny pretended to spit on his hand before he took mine. Well, I *hoped* he was pretending.

No time to worry about it. Because just then . . .
Ka-BAM!

The door to our cabin flew open.

"WELCOME TO CAMP LITTLE DIPPER!" yelled the guy in our doorway. His short, black, bristle-like hair scraped the top of the door opening. And I thought his arms would bust out of the sleeves of his silver coveralls.

Our camp counselor, I presume?

"My name's Alpha Centauri FOUR-POINT-ONE. You can call me COUNSELOR ALPHA."

QUESTION 05:

I give up. What kind of a last name is "Four-Point-One"?

ANSWER 05:

No idea. Maybe his parents worked with computers back in the old days. But Donny was right. He was . . . different.

Anyway, I froze when Counselor Alpha walked in. So did Tag and Mir. Even Zero-G made like a statue at the Lunar Museum of Art.

Not a good start. We were busted—candy, dog, and all.

"It wasn't our fault," said Mir in a tiny voice.

"We didn't mean to," mumbled Tag. "He just stowed away."

"THEODORE ORTIZ." This guy had one setting: LOUD.

"Uh . . . here, sir," Tag squeaked.

"Here with your sister? GOOD. I'm glad you

made it." He acted as if he hadn't heard what we were trying to tell him.

But how did he know our names already? Weird.

"And VLADIMIR CHEKOV?" He turned to Mir. "How is your father?" (Mir's dad was *CLEO-7*'s commander.)

"F-fine, counselor . . . sir."

"DONALD QUANTUM? I see you brought snacks?"

"Uh . . ." Donny gulped. He swallowed his gum wad.

"Well, you're not going to need them here at Camp Little Dipper. You'll get plenty of good vegetables at mealtime. Fresh dome air. And exercise—lots of exercise. Just what humans need."

"Uh-huh."

"And how is LAMAR BRIGHT?"

I nearly fell on my face when he slammed me on the back with a nice, "friendly" pat.

Oooof! "It's Buzz, sir. And about the dog—"

"Don't feel silly, Lamar," he told me. "Lots of campers bring stuffed animals."

Huh? "Oh . . . he's not a stuffed animal." I tried to tell the truth. "He's—"

But Counselor Alpha wasn't listening. He was already jogging out the door, waving us to follow.

"Let's go, Quasars!" (We were the Cabin 02 Quasars.) "Double time! Up the trail."

✳ ✳ ✳

At least we got to know the place, running up and down the cliffs inside the Camp Little Dipper dome. And it was pretty, all right. Especially from up high, looking down on the canyon. The dome was just over our heads, too. We could see through it to Jupiter and the stars past that.

Gorgeous, I thought.

"Maybe," Mir huffed, "we're not as buff as we thought."

Right. This is what we got for living the soft life on a space station.

"Willie's really weary," repeated Tag. "Willie's really weary. Willie's—"

"Who's Willie?" I asked.

Tag shrugged. "It just sounds funny. Willie's really weary. Willie's—"

"Keep RUNNING!" yelled Counselor Alpha.

Donny cheated. He strapped a pair of Delta Pocket Rockets to the bottom of his shoes. That gave him a boost. Otherwise, he would have been as gassed as we were, after an hour and a half of running.

"Cheater!" we told Donny.

"Got an extra pair?" Mir asked.

Donny grinned.

But finally our super-leader brought us back down. And the weird thing was, he wasn't even breathing hard!

"All right, Quasars! Chow time."

Right. We were still gasping for our lives when Super Counselor dragged us into the big eating hall full of kids. But something was strange here, too.

Way strange.

I looked at Mir.

"What's going on, Mir?" I whispered without moving my lips.

Someone at the next table chuckled. They were watching us. And nobody was eating.

"HUNGRY?" Counselor Alpha boomed at us. "HAVE SOME!"

"Sure!" Mir spooned a glob of quivering green goo onto his plate.

"What do you think it is?" Tag asked me. He hadn't tried anything yet. But a minute later, he took a swig of his red juice and—*phfffffft!*—sprayed it across the table.

I hit the floor backward. A couple of kids next to us ducked and laughed.

"Pretty good beet juice, huh?" asked a guy from under the table.

The juice dripped over the edge into my hair. Gross.

"And the quivering stuff?"

"Spinach tofu," he told me.

QUESTION 05:

Tofu, for those of us who don't know, is . . .

ANSWER 05:

Soybean Jell-O. It's supposed to be good for you. But unless it's pizza-flavored, I don't think so . . .

I straightened up and tried to figure out what to do next. By that time, everybody was laughing. Donny had scooped up his tofu in a spoon, looking for a target.

"Hey, kid, want seconds?" he asked a little guy at the end of the table.

Where had Counselor Alpha gone? I had to do something fast, before we had a food riot.

Help! I looked to DeeBee and Miko, sitting at the next table with the girls of Cabin 03.

But they both looked green in the face, too.

Chasing the
5 Bubble Gum Kid ✳ ✳ ✳

Well, needless to say, camp was not turning out to be too stellar. After four days of nonstop vegetables and uphill jogs, I lay in my cabin bunk, trying to go to sleep.

Maybe the spinach juice sloshing in my stomach kept me awake. Or maybe it was just the words to that silly camp yell they made us do after dinner.

Boys: Little Dipper!
Girls: Little Dipper!
Boys: Shoot for the
Girls: STARS!

See what I mean? Pretty lame.

I thought of my good old comfy anti-grav mat at home on *CLEO-7*. And I thought of the good old digital food copier food from the *CLEO-7* dining hall. I even tried counting drones to make myself sleepy.

No go. That didn't help, either.

QUESTION 07:

Wait just a second. Digital food copier?

ANSWER 07:

You remember—a DFC. Back on *CLEO-7*, that's how we make our food.

"Mir, are you asleep?" I whispered.

Mir kept snoring on the bunk below me.

"Mir?" I looked over the edge, and the next thing I knew ... *ka-THUNK!* I was sitting on the cold floor in my Captain Cosmos pajamas.

"Ohhh," I groaned. My tailbone hurt.

Mir turned over but didn't wake up.

"Say there." Zero-G shuffled over for a sniff. "Come to take me out for a midnight run? Donny Quantum wouldn't let me go with him."

"Donny?" I looked over at Donny's bunk. Even in the dark I could tell.

Empty.

"Where did he go?" I wondered out loud.

Zero-G scampered over to the door.

"Let me out, and I'll track him down. Inspector Zero-G to the rescue, my good boy. I'll just follow the scent of his Galaxy Goop. Ready? Ready?"

"Shh. Hold on." I slipped my feet into shoes. "I'm coming."

"Right-oh!" Zero-G was turning circles.

I was dressed and out the door in a nano-second.

That means fast. Way fast.

"Which way?" I shivered when we got outside. Jupiter's shadow filled the dark sky beyond the dome.

Zero-G had his nose to the ground and was off in a flash.

That means fast, too.

"This way." The dog sounded sure of himself.

To tell you the truth, I could have found the way without Zero-G. Maybe it was the trail of candy wrappers in the cold blue light. They led straight to where Mr. Gus had parked our camp shuttle.

"Donny?" I whispered. "Hey, Donnnnn-eeee?"

What was I doing out here, chasing the Bubble Gum Kid?

"Hey, Buzz." That was Mir, coming up behind me. "What are you doing out here?"

Uh-oh. Guess I wasn't as quiet getting out of the cabin as I'd thought.

"Over here." I waved to Mir. And Tag, too. Naturally.

That's when I heard a weird sound coming from inside the shuttle. Something like *ohhh-ah-ha-ha, wah-OOOO!*

"Some kind of animal?" guessed Tag. He was shivering in his pj's.

"Nope." I could see the wrappers leading inside the shuttle's open door.

Zero-G stood by the door and pointed with his paw.

I poked my head inside. "You in here?" By this time, I had a pretty good idea what was going on.

And there he was, sitting at the controls, bawling his eyes out. Donny had his bright orange duffel bag on the floor next to him, and his candy supply, besides.

"What are you doing all dressed?" Tag had to ask.

"Going . . . *sniff, chew, sniff* . . . home." Donny set his big, round jaw and wiped a sleeve across his eyes. "What do you think?"

Only he couldn't figure out how to start the shuttle, I'd bet.

"Long way to go by yourself," said Mir.

"I'm not scared." Donny wasn't fooling anyone.

"Yeah, but if you left," I said, "where would we buy our candy?"

"Hmm." He sniffled. "I hadn't thought of that. Uh, you don't know how to start this thing, do you?"

"Listen, Donny," I told him, "maybe it's not such a good idea."

Donny still wasn't so sure. So we just sat there for a while in the dark, eating his ChocoPlanets and Pluto Pops and telling silly jokes about what we were going to do with the horrible camp food. Tag thought we could paint our faces with the beet juice and use the mushroom burgers to launch an attack against the girls' cabins. After that, Mir told a scary story about giant Io gophers who came out of their holes at night, which wasn't at all true, but it made me think of getting back into bed as fast as we could.

"Just kidding," Mir laughed. "Just kidding."

By that time, we were getting cold, and Tag fell asleep, so I had to carry him piggyback back to the cabin. I almost bumped into Donny and Mir, though, who had stopped just ahead of me.

"I can't believe it," Mir whispered.

Can't believe what?

I looked around him to see what he was talking about.

"Oh no!" I whispered.

Hello Mudda, Hello Fadda

Dear Mom and Dad,

My counselor is a superhuman drill sergeant who makes us jog ten kilometers before breakfast every day. We sat up all last night trying to keep a guy named Donny from running away. The girls raided our cabin. And the food is making everybody sick. Other than that, I'm having a great time. . . .

Day 05, Camp Little Dipper, 0600 hours

(That's six in the morning.)

You should have seen it, frozen underwear all over the roof. We just stood there, stunned.

"Is that yours," Mir nudged me, "with the cute little comets all over?"

I nudged him back and looked around to make sure no one else was awake.

"I sure don't know how they got in and out without waking Counselor Alpha."

"Yeah, well, he sleeps like a dead planet." Donny rested his hands on his hips and shook his head. "Nothing wakes him."

Not even the frozen underwear that slid down the cabin roof just then. Slid down and shattered into a million icicle pieces when it hit the ground.

Talk about cold. Ever seen a pair of underwear do that? I didn't think so.

"Is that you laughing?" Mir asked me.

"I'm not laughing." But I heard it, too. A *snicker-snicker* from somewhere behind us.

"Then . . . who?"

We both turned around to see who was watching us.

"You think freezing someone else's underwear in a subcryonic freezer and tossing them up on a roof is funny, huh?" Mir could sound tough when he wanted to. But he only made them laugh more.

And by that time, I had it figured out.

Who else? Girls!

"We'll get you, DeeBee and Miko," I told them. "When you're not expecting it, we'll get you!"

Day 08, Lake Little Dip, 1500 hours

Three days later, we had our first chance to "get" them—the Camp Little Dipper annual swimming relay race.

"All right, boys, let's show 'em what you can do."

Counselor Alpha's arm muscles bulged when he clapped his hands and yelled at us from the side of the lake.

"Easy for . . . *chomp, smack* . . . him to say." Donny looked worried as he swam around, dog-paddling a few strokes to warm up.

Well, maybe *swam* isn't quite the right word. Actually, he kind of bobbed. But somehow he managed to pull himself back up onto the dock for the race to begin.

So, okay, maybe we didn't do so well in the boys-against-the-girls relay race. Tag did his best, but we were a quarter lap behind coming into the second leg. I did okay, and at the end of my turn we were even with the girls.

"Go, DeeBee!" yelled Tag, and then he clapped his hand over his mouth. "I mean, slow down, DeeBee!"

Didn't make any difference. Mir blew 'em away in the third leg of the race. So we had a huuuuuge lead by the time Donny wound up his arms and launched.

Now, Zero-G had told me to stand back from the lake when Donny jumped in off the dock, but I told him that was rude. And Donny did *not* look like a stranded interplanet freighter.

He just swam like one.

"That's okay, Donny." I clapped him on the back when he finally hauled out. The girls were already jumping up and down and giving each other galactic salutes. (You know, where you hook your little fingers and wave?)

Okay—so maybe sports weren't our thing. But there was always arts and crafts.

Day 11, Little Dipper Craft Hut, 1030 hours

Now, I had to admit, the girls' prank *was* pretty funny. But after six days of frozen underwear jokes . . . well, it was getting a bit old.

"Hey, AstroKids, having a little trouble walking, there?" (Followed by a ha-ha.)

Or, "Yo, AstroBoy, you look a little chilly!" (Followed by a yuk-yuk.)

You get the picture. Things were not the best for the boys of Cabin 02. Especially when DeeBee, Miko, and three other girls peeked in the craft cabin window at us.

You should have heard them giggling.

"Oooo, how come your Jupiter model has a pink moon?" asked one of those other girls.

Huh?

She pointed at a glop that looked sort of like a little planet, but not exactly.

I picked it up, and it stuck to my fingers.

Donny's gum! Gross. How did they get used Galaxy Goop onto my papier-mâché Jupiter?

"Oh, man." Mir tried to help me get it loose, but he only made things worse. "That bubble gum is tearing off half the planet!"

I still couldn't get the big glob of gum off my fingers. And as I pulled, it started to look like a sticky pink spider web.

"There's always the archery challenge," whispered Tag. "We'll do good at *that.*"

Day 14, Little Dipper Archery Range, 1300 hours

"Watch this." Donny squinted and pointed his A.L.G.P.S. at the target.

"I can't even see the bull's-eye," said Mir.

I couldn't, either.

QUESTION 07:

Are you going to tell us what A.L.G.P.S. stands for?

ANSWER 07:

Thought you'd never ask. It stands for *Advanced Laser-Guided Projectile System*. But forget that. Most people would just call it a bow and arrow with a fancy laser scope.

"Don't worry," Donny told us, popping another piece of Galaxy Goop into his mouth. "With this thing, we'll win this competition for sure."

"Is that fair?" Tag wondered out loud.

"Plenty fair."

But just as Donny pulled back on the string and checked his telescope, he blew a giant bubble. And when he let the arrow go, it wasn't a clean *twaang*.

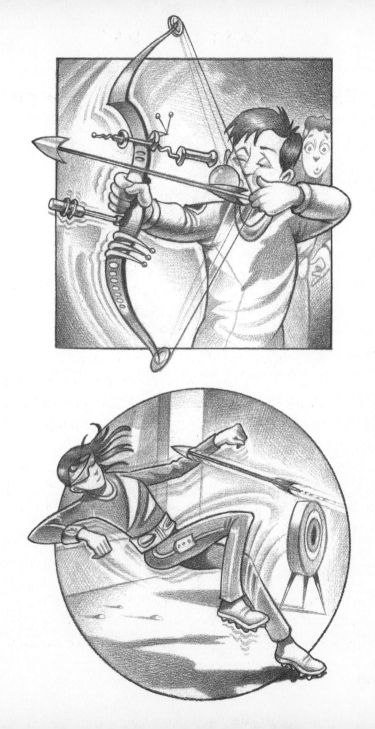

More like a *chew-pop-squish-FWUMP*.

"Look out!" I yelled.

"Runaway projectile!" hollered Mir.

"Loose goop!" added Tag.

As in, wild arrow. People all around the archery course hit the deck—dropped to the ground.

And I closed my eyes when I saw what the arrow was about to hit.

7 Just Add Water ✳ ✳ ✳

Dear Dad and Mom,

My counselor told us the volcano probably won't erupt this year, the way it did last year—which is good. But we can't have archery anymore, on account of that almost-accident with the goopy arrow and the head counselor—which is not good. But don't worry . . .

THWAP!

I don't know how the arrow managed to hit the top part of the lodge. Nowhere near the target. But Donny and I decided it made the lodge look kind of cool. You know, in a rustic, 2175 sort of way?

Only the head counselor, Ursula Minor, didn't quite think so. I bet the arrow didn't come as close to her as she said. (Although I did notice some sticky pink stuff in her hair. . . .)

"I don't understand it!" Donny kept saying as he unwrapped a fresh piece of Galaxy Goop. "The laser was working just fine before."

"Lazy laser ray eraser," mumbled Tag. "Lazy laser ray eraser . . . Say that five times fast. Lazy laser ray eraser, lazy—"

"Ta-ag." I sighed. From backward-talk to tongue twisters. Which was worse?

"BOYS!" Head Counselor Ursula Minor's voice stopped us cold. She and Alpha could have been brother and sister, the way they could holler.

"Yes, ma'am?" I had to say *something*.

"Your laser was miscalibrated by thirty point two millimeters."

"Miss who?" asked Tag.

"Shh," I whispered into his ear. "She means we missed."

Head Counselor Ursula gave us a laser stare. "Cabin 02 will volunteer for extra duty tonight."

Extra duty? That didn't sound real . . .

"All of you will report to the kitchen a half hour before dinner."

"Yes, ma'am," I tried to drown out the sound of Tag's groan and squeezed his arm.

"Hush!" I told him in no-lips mode. "You want to get us in even more trouble?"

But Tag wasn't hearing me.

"I want to go home! I'm tired of camp," he bawled as we escaped back to the cabin.

"Here." Donny stuffed a stick of Luna Licorice into Tag's mouth to keep him quiet. "I'll put it on your account."

That worked for a while. But I was starting to wish I had some of Donny's candy myself when we went to the kitchen that night to serve dinner for everyone.

"Mmmm." Mir held up a plate of food with a grin. "Head Counselor Ursula said that since we were helping, we could have as much food as we wanted."

"Is that our punishment for the arrow thing?" Donny wanted to know.

I took one sniff and nearly lost it again. Maybe it *was*.

"Leaping light-years." I held a hand to my mouth so I wouldn't get sick.

"What is it this time?" asked Tag.

"Protein dogs . . ." Mir held up a kinda sausage thing that kinda wiggled. Nightmare!

"Whatever happened to Jupiter ice cream?" I moaned. "We're so close."

But no chance of that. Besides protein dogs, the menu was prune-and-lima-bean soufflé, with dehydrated water (just add water).

Tag looked at me as if I could help him get out of this mess.

"I have an idea," I told him. "For after dinner."

"If we survive that long," said Donny.

✳ ✳ ✳

We *did* make it—barely. Just after dinner, my stomach was growling a whole lot more than it should have been.

"Last Blast-Off bar." Donny shook one of his bags upside down.

"So what's your idea?" Mir crowded around my bunk with the rest of them.

I dug into the bottom of my duffel bag. "Remember when we were loading the bus, and everybody had to leave stuff behind?" I felt around underneath my three extra pairs of socks for something that felt like a fat wristwatch.

"I'll say." Mir groaned. "They wouldn't even let me take my . . ."

Zingo! I held up my spare wrist interface for everyone to see.

"Well, how about that!" Donny smiled. "You smuggled it in!"

"Not on purpose." I tried to explain. "I was late getting on the shuttle. They didn't check my bag. And I didn't even think about it. But maybe we can call back to *CLEO-7* and—"

"And tell our folks to come get us!" Donny nearly jumped off the bunk.

"Well, I don't know if they'll go for that." I fiddled with the little controls. "But it couldn't hurt to try."

"Good job, old man!" Mir pounded my back until I could hardly breathe. "I knew you'd come through. Buzz Bright to the rescue!"

Donny handed out Root Beer Orbiters to celebrate.

"Not that I'm homesick or anything." He grinned. "But maybe my mom could send me some more, you know . . ."

Yeah. We knew. Donny was down to his last few pieces of Galaxy Goop Double Bubble Gum. And there was still a week of camp left.

"Wait a minute." Tag's face fell. "Aren't we too far away for anybody to hear us?"

Yeah, we *were* far from home. Way far. But I'd already thought of that.

"There's a way to turn off the 3-D picture stuff,"

I told him. "That should boost the power to the voice signal. I don't think we can get a message back, but maybe we can send one."

"Kind of like praying." Mir was joking.

"Nope." I shook my head. "God hears. With wrist interfaces, we have no idea if our folks are going to hear."

"But . . ." Tag wasn't quite sure. "I thought you said you can make it work."

"Well, we might need a little help."

And there was only one place to get it.

"You don't mean—" Mir's jaw went *thunk*, like it dropped out of gear. I knew that he knew that I knew what he was thinking.

"You're not saying . . ." Tag was catching on, too.

But this was an emergency.

"Yup." I nodded. "I'm saying it."

So forget about getting the girls back for all their tricks and bad jokes. I took a deep breath and said: "DeeBee would know."

Was I kidding? Are you kidding?

DeeBee! The GEEN-ius!

She was our only chance.

 ## 8 S.O.S.

$* * *$

Dear Mom and Dad,

Today we learned to cook mushroom burgers over a little volcano, and our counselor showed us a neat new way to roast soymallows. It works pretty well, although Tag is going to look weird until his hair grows back. . . .

"Boys." DeeBee grinned when she had my spare wrist interface taken apart. "You're helpless sometimes."

"No, we're not." Count on Tag to argue with his sister. "We knew what we wanted to do. And we knew who could help us do it."

Right. That's not helpless.

DeeBee shook her head. "Well, I'm not much help to you."

No help?

"No. I can't do it without a power boost from

somewhere. This camp has *nothing*."

"Oh, but I think it does, Mistress DeeBee. Allow me, if you please." Zero-G sniffed around the floor of our cabin until he had snuffled into a closet. We looked at each other and shrugged. But a minute later, he came out with something in his mouth.

"Oh, these things *do* taste horrid." Zero-G sounded as disgusted as a dog could sound.

"What do you have there?" I got down on my knees to find out.

Zero-G dropped a small silver disk on the floor and waggled his tongue.

"Rrrr-UFFF! TOO-eey. YUK!"

A tri-lithium battery?

He dropped it at our feet as if it were a moon gopher or a half-chewed blaster slipper. And he stood there, wagging his tail, waiting for us to pat him on the head or tell him he was a good space doggy.

"I do hope this is what you're looking for, Miss DeeBee." Zero-G kept shaking his head, his tongue hanging out.

"Perfect!" DeeBee pounced on the battery and held it up to the light. "It just might work."

We didn't try to figure out where the battery had

come from. Tri-lithiums were usually only for drones and robotics. Right now it was good enough to watch DeeBee do her miracle on my wrist interface. We even convinced Zero-G to find us a few more batteries.

"Only if it means getting some proper food." He licked his lips. "I must confess I'm terribly hungry."

"Sure you don't want some tofu?" Donny asked him. "We could find you some."

"Donny!" DeeBee didn't look away from her project. "Dogs don't eat that kind of thing."

"We're intelligent, after all." Zero-G was intelligent, all right. Meaning, smart.

Meaning, maybe smarter than all us AstroKids put together.

"Stand up straighter, Mir." DeeBee pointed up. "Hold your right arm out."

Mir did as he was told. By that time, DeeBee had him wired up pretty well. And when he held out both his hands, maybe we could get this puppy to work.

A human antenna.

"Hear anything yet?" Tag squirmed next to his sister.

She leaned closer to the wrist interface on the table and shook her head.

"I think we can send a message," she finally whispered, "but I don't know if we'll be able to hear anything back."

"Cool!" Tag leaned closer and pushed a button on the interface. "Testing. TESTING. One, two, three! Mom! Dad! This is Tag. We need you to come get us, quick! We're gonna starve at this—"

"Tag!" DeeBee pulled her brother back from the interface. "Cut it out. Every time you talk, it drains the batteries. And . . . Oh no."

She groaned and fiddled with the control again. A red light faded, then blinked out.

"Just from talking?" Tag's jaw dropped. "I didn't mean to."

"Let me do it next time, okay?" She tapped at the battery. "It's really touchy."

"More batteries?" I looked at Mir and Donny. We all looked at Zero-G.

"Now, wait a minute." Zero-G started to back away. "Do you have any idea how bad-awful-horrible that battery tasted?"

"You don't have to *eat* 'em, Zero-G." Mir

laughed and put down his antenna arms. "Just find us some more."

"Or I could get you some tofu." Donny shrugged his shoulders.

"Right-oh. I'm on it." Our super-dog went on the chase once more.

Just in time, too. Because as soon as Zero-G left to sniff out some more batteries, Counselor Alpha came busting through the door, *ka-boom*, the way he always did.

"Well, THERE you are." He dumped a half-dozen backpacks on the floor. "READY TO GO?"

Suffering satellites! Could somebody turn down the volume on that guy?

Tag and Mir stood up straight, their backs to the table. There was no telling what might happen if Counselor Alpha found the wrist interface.

"Go?" Tag's eyes were already wide.

"Where to?" Mir finished the sentence.

"Did you forget?" Counselor Alpha rested his hands on his hips, drill-sergeant style.

I scratched my head, too. Yet another double-time jog around Io wearing heavy weights on our backs? *Please . . . no!*

"We're camping out on the top of Mount Ion

tonight. We leave at 1800. The Cabin 02 Quasars and the Cabin 03 Comets."

"Tell my folks I croaked with clean socks on," I whispered, pulling on my boots.

Overnighter
9 Disaster

Dear Mom and Dad,

You can tell Mr. and Mrs. Chekhov that Mir is okay now. Who knew that a little cut on the head could bleed so much?.

"Warning, warning!" Everybody laughed when Tag hunched his shoulders and waved his arms. "The station's digital food copiers are about to blow!"

More laughing. You'd think we'd never seen anybody pretending to be a station drone, floating around and acting totally dorky.

"Don't worry!" This time it was Mir's turn to make us laugh, with his squeaky high voice. "I'm DeeBee Ortiz, and I can fix anything on the station. Here, let me show you."

Even DeeBee was laughing at the skit. Maybe it was the silly string wig Mir was wearing, with a braid on each side of his face.

Tag was almost rolling on the ground, he thought it was so funny. Like, "This is even better than the spit around the planet skit!"

I hope so. Of course, out here, camped way up on Mount Ion, right near the top of the dome, just about everything seemed funnier. Don't ask me why.

But you know how people get the giggles. Miko sure had 'em when she got up in front of everybody. The only light was a flickering red lava pool a few yards away.

"And now, (giggle) ladies and gentlemen, Miss DeeBee Ortiz (giggle) is going to fix all the food copiers on the station, while our fearless (giggle) AstroKids leader, Buzz, is going to serve us the best meal you've ever tasted!"

Everybody laughed when my stomach growled.

Miko bowed and moved to the side just in time.

Because, *ka-POW!*

We all jumped from where we were sitting on rocks and stuff. You know, like when someone comes up behind you and pops a big paper bag? That's what it sounded like. Only this was no paper bag.

"Ow! What happened?" Mir must have jumped the most. I think he even scraped his head on the side of a boulder.

"Are you okay?" DeeBee was laughing, and she bent over to help him.

"I'm fine." Mir held the back of his head and looked around. "But—"

"Did the food copiers all blow up?" asked Tag. Maybe he thought it was all part of the skit.

"Just a little volcano vent." DeeBee pointed.

QUESTION 09:
> Okay, time to explain. You're sitting on *top* of a volcano?

ANSWER 08:
> Pretty much. Did I tell you this little moon of Jupiter's is covered with volcano vents? There's always something brewing on Io!

Just a little volcano vent. Well, that was a relief. Wasn't even enough to wake up Counselor Alpha. We could still see his boots sticking out of his tent. The guy could sleep through anything!

But the volcano vents bubbling, the digital food

copier skit . . . it all gave me an idea.

"You mean there are *other* ways to heat up food?" Tag couldn't believe me. "Not just digital food copiers?"

"I say we try it." Donny was ready to eat anything. Most of the other kids were, too.

"Okay, so here's what we do. . . ." I showed them how to get sticks and poke the ends into the mushroom-burger patties we had to bring. Then we gathered around the lava pool and held them out over the hottest spots. And pretty soon . . .

"It's working!" said Donny. His burger was burnt to a black crisp. But hey, he looked happy. "I say we have Buzz fix the food back at the camp, too!"

Right. Barbecued space beets and char-burnt Brussels sprouts.

"How did you know how to do this, Buzz?" Mir wanted to know.

I shrugged. "Just an old cowboy vid I saw once. Watch out for more burps from the lava, though."

We *did* watch out. That didn't help us any, though, when the ground started rumbling under our feet.

"Cool." (Tag thought everything was cool.) "Earthquakes."

Well, sort of cool. When it happened again, we all popped up and yelped. You know, like you do during a Lunarland roller coaster ride?

"Whooooaaaaaa!"

Only this wasn't a ride. And Counselor Alpha was still sleeping through it all. After a few minutes of shaking, Tag and a few others gave up hollering at him.

"I don't think this is so cool anymore," he said. "I want to go home."

"Yeah." Some of the other kids nodded their heads, too.

"What about the wrist interface?" Miko asked. "Can we try it again?"

The ground shook, and DeeBee nodded her head. "As soon as we get back to camp."

"Hey, everybody." This time Mir had an idea. "Want to hear a scary story?"

Now? You've got to be kidding!

A barbecued mushroom burger hit him right in the nose.

Galaxy Goop
10 Stew

✳ ✳ ✳

Dear Dad,

You'd be proud of me. And you'd never guess how much money I've earned here at camp. More than washing space shuttles back home! And just for sticking my head in a bowl of cream of turnip soup that nobody wanted to eat. . . .

We almost didn't get down off Mount Ion the next morning.

Not because of all the earthquakes. Well, they were bad enough! Ever tried running down a hill made of Jell-O? Earthquakes feel a little like that.

But it was more than that.

Actually, if you have to blame someone, blame Mir. I told him to forget it. But no.

"Come on, Buzz," he whispered from the other side of the tent at 0600 hours. "Remember the frozen underwear?"

Boy, did I. So I followed Mir outside, and we sneaked up on the girls' tents, about a hundred yards away.

Mir was chuckling to himself. "This is going to be perfect."

"What's going to be perfect?"

Mir held up a big, slobbery blob about twice the size of his thumb.

"Where'd you get that slug?" I asked.

"Shh." He held up a finger to his lips.

"You're not going to—"

Mir nodded.

"Mir!" I grabbed his arm. "Don't!"

But by that time, I couldn't stop him from sneaking into one of the tents. I watched as he laid the slug right over DeeBee's lips.

Oh no!

"Hehehehehehe!" Mir shot out of the tent and ran back to ours. "This is going to be sooooo good."

"Sooooo good" was not what I would call it.

First we heard a *mmm-mmm* groaning, like DeeBee was kind of talking in her sleep.

Then a deep breath.

Then a bit of lip-smacking.

Then a scream like you've never heard before.

And now you know what made coming down the mountain so tough.

"I still can't *believe* you let him do that to me!" DeeBee hit my shoulder—again—as we were hiking back to the lodge. At least she was still speaking with me. "I thought you were my friend."

"I *am* your friend."

"Well, friends don't let friends eat slugs."

"Look, I'm really sorry." I was huffing and puffing again. Which was no surprise, since Counselor Alpha was leading the way. "I didn't know what he was doing."

Which was true.

"Yeah, well, maybe we can duplicate a special slug stew for Mir when we get back."

"We'll see." I didn't think so. But when I thought of it, what could be worse than what we were going to have to eat?

"We're having liver tofu and chopped Martian eggplant," Counselor Alpha told us a few minutes later. "You'll love it. It's good for human units."

Human units? Huh? I felt more like a hunger unit. My knees started to wobble. That's how I get when I'm in the last stages of starvation. I had to do something about the terrible food at Camp Little Dipper.

But what?

Then I had an idea. A long shot, maybe, but—

"DeeBee and I will help in the kitchen tonight," I told Counselor Alpha.

"Wonderful." He didn't slow down. "You can help shred the eggplant and fix something good."

"Uh, sure."

"Wait a minute!" I think DeeBee nearly had a heart attack.

"Trust me," I whispered, and a half hour later I dragged her with me to the kitchen. They gave us aprons and funny white hats to wear while we worked. An older, heavy-duty digital food copier filled up a whole wall.

QUESTION 09:
> This is how the camp workers made all that *delicious* turnip and lima bean and beet and tofu stuff?

ANSWER 09:
> You got it.

"We're going to fix something good," I told her.

DeeBee shook her head. "But all we can do is copy what they have. And all they have are vegetables and a few dried fruits."

Right. Copying is what DFCs do.

"We can't make milkshakes out of Brussels sprouts." Sensible DeeBee again.

"I know that." I reached into my pocket. "But check it out. Counselor Alpha said we should fix something good."

DeeBee stared at the piece of Galaxy Goop gum in my hand, and I think the light went on in her head, too.

"Bubble gum pie," I whispered.

"Bubble gum stew."

"Bubble gum pudding."

"Bubble gum waffles."

"Bubble gum . . ."

We could have come up with a thousand and one new ways to fix bubble gum.

"Wait a minute, Buzz." DeeBee still wasn't so sure.

"What?" I started to adjust the controls.

"There's something funny about this food copier."

I wasn't sure what she meant. It was just a little

older than what we were used to. I keyed in a new code for the timer.

1-3-3-0 . . . I think. We'd have to make a few changes for bubble gum stew.

"Hmm." I scratched my head. "Maybe the controls in this closet over here will work better."

So I checked out the big control closet. I was pretty sure it tied in to the food copier. Anyway, it had a bunch of little green blinking lights and a dozen orange view screens. Each screen was filled with numbers and funny writing, like *P/SYS 002, variable$, 33K.*

Right. I could figure it out. All I had to do was switch the food code. So I punched a few more buttons, changed a few more numbers. But that didn't seem to do anything.

"That's a warning light, Buzz." DeeBee was looking over my shoulder. "I think maybe you should let me . . ."

Uh-oh. The little green blinking lights had turned to little *red* blinking lights.

Not good.

Then a buzzer went off.

Really not good.

That's when we heard everybody out in the dining hall start to holler and shout. Had the bubble gum stew come through already?

I had a bad feeling it was something else.

Something a lot worse.

Counselors
11 Unplugged

* * *

Dear Mom,

You should see the cool-looking snakes they have here on Io. I'll have plenty of room in my suitcase to bring one home, since all my underwear is gone. See you soon. . . .

Forget frozen underwear. This was serious.

But with all the yelling in the dining room, I couldn't even hear myself think. Finally, though, I could tell what was going on.

"Look at this!" Mir moved his hand back and forth in front of Counselor Alpha's stiff face. "They're all robots. And their program must've crashed."

Oh, man. DeeBee came running out to see. What had I done? The control closet must not have been linked to the digital food copier, after all, but some kind of robot control center. Weird.

It seemed unreal, but Mir was right. Kids were crowding around each counselor, poking at them just to make sure. All the Little Dipper staff were like statues.

"Wake up, Counselor Alpha." Tag poked at the poor guy's side with his fork.

Counselor Alpha didn't blink.

"I *knew* there was something funny with this place." DeeBee shook her head. "I just can't believe I didn't see it. And I can't believe they fooled us."

But now it all made sense. The spare robotic batteries that Zero-G found. The way Counselor Alpha wouldn't wake up when he was sleeping. (It must have been his cold recharge time.) The "human unit" talk . . .

But never mind all that. I had to go fix the controls before things got out of hand.

"Yee-haw!" Donny jumped up on a table, stepping in a plate full of Brussels sprout casserole. "Throw out your tofu. It's party time!"

"No, wait a minute." I put up my hands, but no one noticed me. You could have heard them cheering all the way to Jupiter.

"I'll go back to the kitchen and try to fix it,"

DeeBee shouted into my ear. "You keep things calm here."

Right. *If anyone listens.*

Donny was starting a combo food-fight/dance. I tried to grab his arm, but I slipped and fell on some healthy slime food.

"Wait, Donny!"

No use. Where were Miko and Mir and Tag?

"Bubble gum for dinner!" yelled Donny.

Cheers.

"Double dessert!"

Triple cheers.

"No bedtime!"

By this time, most of the campers were going berserk. You know, bonkers?

Nuts.

Wacko.

Finally, I managed to grab Donny's shirt in the food-fight mess.

"Donny, cool it. Don't you see what you're doing?"

Donny looked at me as if I were from Pluto.

"Hey, no counselors, no rules. What are you worried about? We're finally going to have some fun, Mr. AstroKid!"

"No, you don't get it, Donny. You can't just go wild."

"I can't?" Donny was being swept away by the crowd. "Watch me."

No thanks. As soon as we could find everyone, we had an emergency AstroKids meeting in the kitchen. Right in the middle of all the frozen camp-staff robots.

"This is really creepy." Mir grunted as he leaned one more against the kitchen wall. I counted Counselor Alpha and Head Counselor Ursula Minor and twenty-seven others, all frozen stiff. I don't mean frozen *cold* stiff like our underwear. I mean stiff stiff. Some had their mouths open, others were pointing their fingers or had their arms crossed. Like they were frozen in time.

Way creepy.

"But look at this." Miko leaned closer to one of the robots, a woman counselor. "Perfect skin, perfect hair . . ."

"Now we know how Counselor Alpha could keep running so much." Mir nodded.

Right. Plenty of fresh tri-lithium batteries.

"I'm really sorry," I told them as I paced. "This

is all my fault. I shouldn't have messed with the controls."

"Don't worry about it." DeeBee waved her hand.

"Yeah, but can't we fix it?" Tag asked.

"There's some kind of phasic timer," DeeBee explained. "It won't let me restart for at least another twenty-four hours."

I moaned. Twenty-four more hours of Donny's Wild Adventure? Camping out on Mount Ion with no food and no water and no blankets would be better.

"But we'll keep sending our help message," she said. "Maybe somebody back home on *CLEO-7* will hear us."

"I doubt it." I frowned.

"But you're the one who said God always hears us, Buzz." Leave it to Tag to remind me.

"I know, but—"

"But what?"

But my stomach was feeling worse and worse. And it didn't get much better over the next few hours. Because, face it: We were stuck on Io with a bunch of dead robots and a hundred-some crazy campers.

None of the AstroKids were going to get much

sleep that night, either. Instead, DeeBee sent a few more S.O.S. messages.

And believe me, we prayed a lot.

"Buzz?" That was Tag, about 0200. Two in the morning.

"Go to sleep, Tag."

"Buzz?" Tag, about 0300. Three in the morning.

"You really ought to try to sleep, Tag."

"Buuuuzzzz!" Try 0400.

Oh, man.

"Something smells really bad, Buzz."

"I told you, you need to take a hypershower every day. If you don't—"

"No, I don't mean that kind of smell. I mean, it smells like rotten eggs out there!"

Ahhhh-OOOOO!

What a howl! The hair on the back of my neck stood up.

"Is that a wolf?" Mir bumped his head when he sat up.

"Of course not." I flipped on the light. "It's just— hey, quit shaking my bed, Tag."

"I'm n-not shaking your bed." Tag wasn't kidding. He was shivering on his own bed. What?

The door crashed open. Then I smelled it, too.

And believe me, this smell didn't tap you on the shoulder.

It knocked you in the face! Whew!

"Buzz!" yelled DeeBee, who had raced over from Cabin 03. "Guys. We've got big trouble."

More than what we already had?

A piece of the ceiling dropped to my feet.

Ka-BOOM!

And one of the windows popped out.

Ka-RASH! Tinkle, tinkle.

"Everybody out of the cabin!" I yelled.

Buzz Takes 12 Charge   * * *

Dear Mom and Dad,

I'm really sorry about the mess we've made here at Camp Little Dipper. I didn't mean to, honest. But it all started with the Galaxy Goop Double Bubble Gum. . . .

Okay, this is where everything happened so fast I could hardly tell you what happened first, then second or third. It was just *bam-bam-bam*.

But let me try.

Okay, first, we ran out of that cabin as fast as we could. Zero-G pulled on Tag's leg to get him to hurry up. (That's what the "wolf" call was. Zero-G.)

Next, we got everybody out in front of the main lodge. Out! Out! Out! And now it was time for someone to really take charge.

"Go ahead, Buzz." DeeBee pushed me up in

front of the crowd. "They'll listen to you now."

Maybe. I whistled loudly, and everybody got quiet, even Donny and his crazy campers.

"All right," I yelled. "Listen up!"

"What's that yukky smell?" A girl held her nose.

"The volcanoes," explained DeeBee. "They're venting."

"And they're gonna blow!" yelled Tag. "This whole moon's gonna blow!"

"Tag!" His sister cut him short. "You don't know that."

Maybe not. But it didn't look too good to me, either. I took a deep breath and choked on the rotten egg volcano smell. And then we heard it again. . . .

Ka-POP!

Yikes! We all jumped and covered our heads.

"This is it!" Tag screamed.

But when we looked around a few seconds later, we were still alive. And Donny was peeling a huge Galaxy Goop bubble off his cheeks.

"Sorry," he mumbled.

"We don't have time to fool around," I decided. Galaxy Goop or no Galaxy Goop, this was not good. Where could we go . . . before Camp Little Dipper was toast?

"Maybe we should call for help again," said Mir.

The ground rumbled once more. Had anybody heard our calls before? I didn't think so.

"This is what we're going to do," I told them. "We're getting out of here. Everybody head for the shuttle."

But once we got to the old space bus, we all stood there and stared.

Double whoops.

"Uh, Buzz?" said Miko. "You think we're all going to fit on that thing . . . at the same time?"

Good question. And please don't ask me why there weren't more shuttles. Actually, there *was* another one leaning up against a shed, but it was all in pieces.

"Oh, man," Mir mumbled. "Where's Gus A. Paulow when you need him?"

I didn't want to tell him, but the old shuttle pilot was over behind the broken shuttle—as "frozen" as the rest of the staff. Who knew he was robotic, too?

"All right, everybody! Listen up." I stood at the door and yelled out over the faces. One hundred and twenty-three faces, plus Zero-G, stared back at me, waiting.

Each of them wanted a seat. Problem was, there were only forty seats on the shuttle. You can do the math.

Gulp. I hoped my stomach would be okay.

"It's going to be a little crowded," I told them, "but we're all going to get on this thing."

Did I say *a little* crowded? More like wall-2-wall, nose-2-nose kids. And did you know some of the kids hadn't taken a hypershower since they got to camp? Gross.

"One hundred twenty-one, one hundred twenty-two . . ." A couple minutes later, I pushed one last kid through the door.

FIIIZLE-pop! By now, the volcanoes in the hills around us were upchucking for sure. But who had time to think? I crawled in over Donny and whistled for Zero-G. "C'mon, pup!"

"The doors, Miko!" I yelled. No time to waste. "Shut the doors!"

And I hoped Miko would know how to drive this thing.

"You *do* know how, don't you?"

Miko waved her hand, checked out the controls,

and started punching buttons. The right ones, I hoped.

Whoo-whoo-weee . . . went the thrusters. I remembered that sound from before. Also the pops and the poofs. So far, so good.

"Is that a volcano?" asked a guy next to me. (His chin was pressed into my back.)

Our floor tilted, and we almost fell over.

"Hold on!" I yelled. "We're taking off!"

Hold on to what? Nobody could move anyway. And the shuttle just kept rocking and rolling.

"Miko?" I looked over at our pilot.

"Doing the best I can!" For once, she didn't look so calm.

That's when I saw the antimatter pods hanging out of the ceiling. Only this time, they were all split up—and glowing brighter all the time. No wonder we weren't going anywhere! I had to do something—fast.

"Give me your gum, Donny. Quick."

"Huh?" Donny choked and swallowed. "No!"

I pounded him on the back as hard as I could and held out my hand. All of a sudden, I was holding a wad the size of your fist.

I know. Gross. But what else could hold together the pods? I sort of clamped them together with the wad, like glue.

But then I couldn't get my *hands* unstuck!

"Try it again, Miko."

That might have done the trick if the giant Little Dipper dome hadn't decided to fold in on us. You've been inside a tent when someone pulls the ropes?

"The whole thing is tearing apart!" Miko squinted and pushed the Go stick all the way to the floor.

Zoooo-WHOINK! Finally, our old shuttle's thrusters kicked in, and everybody got scrunched toward the back. Would we make it out before the bubble came crashing down on us?

QUESTION 10:

Well, you're not going to leave us hanging, are you?

ANSWER 10:

Leaping light-years! Leave you hanging? No way!

At first, I thought it was all over. All I could see

out the front window was a big sheet of clear plexi-dome, falling right on top of us.

"Ay-EEE!" hollered Tag. A couple of girls screamed in my ears, too.

All I could do was hang on. Remember? My hands were still gum-stuck.

But you should have seen it. Should have *felt* it.

Fooo-WHOOOSH! The antimatter thrusters finally did their thing, and . . .

"Hey, look at that!" When Tag pointed, he poked me in the eye. Ow! But I hardly noticed. I just held my breath and stared at . . .

"Stars!" yelled someone else. Beautiful, bright stars and planets and all that good stuff.

Meaning, we were free!

Yes! Everybody started clapping and cheering. Everybody except me. (Remember my gummy hands?)

The thrusters worked. Galaxy Goop Double Bubble Gum really *was* good for something, after all. Ask Donny. I decided if I ever got my fingers unstuck from those antimatter pods (when we got home), I was going to shake his hand.

Good thing we were only ten million kilometers from *CLEO*-7. Tag figured we'd be there quicker than you could say "seven slick slimy sliding snakes" ten times fast. (Go ahead, try it!)

Speaking of which, after a couple of hours, Tag was still crawling around between people's legs, looking for . . .

"Here, snakey-snakey," he whispered.

"What did you say?" A girl next to me lifted her feet, and her face turned white.

"I lost my Ionian gopher snakes," he answered. "I'm bringing a couple home as a present for Mom. They don't bite. Just don't step on them, okay?"

"Ohh," groaned DeeBee. She held her head. "Tag, when we get home, things are going to be different."

"What do you mean?" I asked.

"I don't know. Just different. You'll see."

Okay. But it was going to be a long trip home, snakes and all.

I did feel bad, though, about leaving behind all those robo-counselors at Camp Little Dipper. We didn't even get to say good-bye!

"Yeah," DeeBee told me. "And if they ever wake up, they're sure going to wonder what happened."

One thing was sure, though: If we'd stayed back

on Io just a few minutes longer, we'd be off-line, too.

Oh well. You know we did try to call for help. But we found out later our parents never got the message. I guess we were too far away, after all.

The neat part is that we weren't too far away for God to hear. He didn't even need a wrist interface! And wow, He sure answered us, too.

No kidding! I thought of that—with a few inter-ruptions from Tag—as we zipped home. He never did find his snakes. (Which was probably just as well for Mrs. Ortiz!) Tag still drove us crazy, though, when he challenged everybody to say "Richard's wretched ratchet wrench" ten times fast. Richard's wretched . . . oh, forget it.

And then Miko started up another round of "Ninety-Nine Bottles of Saturn Soda on the Wall."

We'll be home by dinnertime, I promised myself. *If I have to get out and push!*

RealSpace
Debrief

* * *

Jumping Jupiter!

Maybe you've seen a map of the solar system. You know, with the sun in the middle and all the planets twirling around it?

Well, a lot of those maps aren't quite right. The planets are spread out, waaay far apart. But of course, if you did a map just right, you'd hardly be able to see the little planets. They're that far apart!

That's only part of the story. The other part is how big those planets really are compared to one another. And since *The Cosmic Camp Caper* takes place near Jupiter, let's talk about that planet for a minute.

The fifth planet from the sun (Earth is the third) is by far the biggest that we know of. How big? Blow up a beach ball. Then set a marble next to it. The beach ball is Jupiter. The marble is Earth.

That's how big.

Jupiter also has a whole bunch of moons. So many, in fact, that astronomers with heavy-duty telescopes are still discovering new ones. At last count (in the year 2001), the number was up to twenty-eight. They'll probably find more. Some are about the same size as Earth's moon; others are only a couple of kilometers across. As DeeBee would say, BCOR. Big Chunks of Rock.

Jupiter's moons have funny names, too, like Ganymede, Europa, Callisto, and . . . Io! A lot of them are named after characters in old Greek myths.

And this is where it gets really interesting. Io may even have an atmosphere. Not enough to breathe, but it's there. Io's also the one with volcanoes spitting sulfur into the air. (Phew!) In fact, it's the most active "volcano-y" body in the entire solar system!

Funny how excited some scientists get about Jupiter's moons, though. Just like the scientists who want to explore Mars, some of them want to someday explore Jupiter's moons. They think maybe they'll find life in water under Europa's ice. Or clues about how life started.

Well, just check out Isaiah 40:26 in your Bible,

where God says, "Look up to the skies. Who created all these stars?"

You don't need to go all the way to Jupiter to find the answer to *that* question!

Just read on to the next couple of verses to learn more.

Want to find out more about space? Then check out a great Web site for kids called "The Space Place." The address is *www.spaceplace.jpl.nasa.gov.* You can do space experiments there, discover amazing space facts, and lots more.

And the Coded Message Is... ✳ ✳ ✳

You think this ASTROKIDS adventure is over? Not yet. Here's the plan: We'll give you the directions, you find the words. Write them all on a piece of paper. They form a secret message that has to do with *The Cosmic Camp Caper*. If you think you got it right, log on to *www.bethanyhouse.com* and follow the instructions there. You'll receive free ASTROKIDS wallpaper for your computer and a sneak peek at the next ASTROKIDS adventure. It's that simple!

WORD 1:
chapter 7, paragraph 52, word 6   _____

WORD 2:
chapter 11, paragraph 16, word 4   _____

WORD 3:
chapter 5, paragraph 8, word 35   _____

WORD 4:
chapter 7, paragraph 9, word 8 _____

WORD 5:
chapter 6, paragraph 2, word 16 _____

WORD 6:
chapter 10, paragraph 17, word 4 _____

WORD 7:
chapter 1, paragraph 1, word 3 _____

WORD 8:
chapter 5, paragraph 43, word 10 _____

WORD 9:
chapter 2, paragraph 11, word 4 _____

WRITE IT ALL HERE:

_____

_____

(Hint: Ever read 1 John? Give it a try!)

Contact Us! ✳ ✳ ✳

If you have any questions for the author or would just like to say hi, feel free to contact him at Bethany House Publishers, 11400 Hampshire Avenue South, Bloomington, MN 55438, United States of America, EARTH. Please include a self-addressed, stamped envelope if you'd like a reply. Or log on to Robert's intergalactic Web site at *www.coolreading.com*.

Launch Countdown

* * *

AstroKids 07:
The Super-Duper Blooper

Lights, camera, action—the AstroKids have been discovered!

At least it looks that way when famous holo-vid producer Neta Neutron descends on *CLEO-7* to screen test DeeBee Ortiz and the other AstroKids.

Great, but how did someone so famous find out about them? Soon DeeBee learns that Mir sent in a recording of her and the other AstroKids clowning around in her workshop. And the rest, as they say, is history.

Actually, the rest of the AstroKids are history. It doesn't take long for Neta to tell them that only DeeBee has the right stuff to take a turn at being co-hostess of Neta's top-rated holo-vid show. A star is born!

But life as a superstar isn't what DeeBee thought it would be. Worse yet, her big chance might really cost her. Is the price worth it? Or will DeeBee's show become a super blooper?

THE CUL-DE-SAC KIDS

Visit the Cul-de-sac for Fun and Faith

A former school teacher, Beverly Lewis knows what children love to read–fun and funny stories starring kids just like them. As a mother and grandmother, though, she understands how important it is for books to teach Godly lessons.

Her CUL-DE-SAC KIDS series is a winner for both kids and parents. Introducing a cast of lovable neighborhood children, every book is an adventure as the gang solves mysteries and learns valuable lessons about faith.

⬙ BETHANYHOUSE

11400 Hampshire Ave. S. • Minneapolis, MN 55438 • 1-800-328-6109 • www.bethanyhouse.com